MUSH'S
Jazz
Adventure

Pinkwater's guides to the galaxy

MUSH'S Jazz Adventure

WRITTEN BY DANIEL PINKWATER
ILLUSTRATED BY JILL PINKWATER

Aladdin Paperbacks

New York London Toronto Sydney Singapore

First Aladdin Paperbacks edition November 2002

Text copyright © 2002 by Daniel Pinkwater
Illustrations copyright © 2002 by Jill Pinkwater

ALADDIN PAPERBACKS
An imprint of Simon & Schuster Children's Publishing Division
1230 Avenue of the Americas, New York, NY 10020

Designed by Lisa Vega
The text of this book was set in Cheltenham Book.
Printed in the United States of America
2 4 6 8 10 9 7 5 3 1

Library of Congress Control Number 2001056085
ISBN 0-689-84572-3 (Aladdin pbk.)

Contents

My Best Friend

I am Kelly Mangiaro. My dog is the only dog in the world who knows how to cook and talk. She is not an ordinary dog. She is a mushamute, a dog from another planet. No one knows these things about her. Only I know. Her name is Mush. She is my best friend.

Mush takes care of me while my parents are at work. They think she is a trustworthy dog, which she is. They do not know she can talk, or cook. They think I am learning to cook, which I am. Mush is teaching me.

Mush and I spend a lot of time in the woods. The woods start just behind our house, which is the last house on the street. It's interesting walking in the woods with Mush. She notices things. She says she has an educated nose. Really, she is educated all over.

"Notice! There are raccoons sleeping in this tree," Mush said one day.

"Where? I can't see them," I said.

"Watch the leaves move in the breeze," Mush said. "When the leaves move this way, you see a tiny bit of raccoon, and when they move that way, you see another tiny bit. After a while you can figure out the whole shape."

When Mush speaks to me, I usually hear her voice in my head—and she can hear what I am thinking too. She can speak out loud, but

she is hard to understand when she does that. Sometimes when I am with Mush in the woods, I can hear what other animals are saying. I think I pick it up from Mush's brain.

"Mommy, what kind of animals are those down below?" I heard a raccoon say.

"It's a wolf or dog of some sort, and a human," I heard the raccoon mother say. "Very dangerous. Just stay still. They won't see us."

"Sorry to wake you," Mush said. "My friend and I are just taking a walk and studying nature. We mean you no harm."

"That's very nice," the raccoon mother said. "Naturally, I believe every word you say . . . NOT!"

"I assure you, we are completely peaceful," Mush said.

"We will stay up here in the tree, just the same, thank you," the mother raccoon said.

"As you wish," Mush said. "We will continue our walk."

"Very suspicious, that raccoon," Mush said to me, as we walked along.

"Well, you can't blame her," I said. "People have been known to hunt them with guns and dogs."

"Whatever for?" Mush asked.

"I don't know."

"Well, next time we come this way, let's bring them a banana."

"A banana?" I asked.

"Raccoons are crazy about bananas. It will be a gesture of friendship."

A Picnic

W e came to a little open place in the woods. There was soft green grass, and it was bright with sun.

"This would be a good place to have our lunch," Mush said. "Are you hungry?"

"I am," I said.

"So am I," Mush said. "Tell me what you prepared for lunch."

Mush had allowed me to fix a lunch all by myself, and I was carrying it in a paper bag.

"I have three kinds of sandwiches: sliced cucumbers and butter, peanut butter and sliced strawberries on whole wheat, and cream cheese with black pepper and honey." These were all sandwiches Mush had taught me to make.

"A nice selection," Mush said. "Did you cut the crusts off the bread?"

Mush likes picnic sandwiches with the crusts cut off. I myself like the crust, but Mush says as long as I am her cooking pupil, I have to do things her way.

"What else did you bring?"

"Two pieces of carrot cake, two apples, and a bottle of lemonade," I told Mush.

"And a cloth?"

"Yes, I have a large napkin to spread on the ground."

"Satisfactory," Mush said. "I think this is a good spot, don't you?"

Of course, this was just a little bag lunch for a walk in the woods. When Mush plans a full-size picnic, things can get very fancy.

Mush nibbled her sandwiches. She is a very delicate eater for such a large dog. She allowed me to bite into my apple, but she peeled hers with a little knife and cut it into slices.

I liked eating my lunch in the sunshine with Mush and drinking lemonade out of a paper cup. Mush put her great nose up into the breeze and sniffed deeply.

"There is nothing so nice as lunching in the woods," Mush said. "It reminds me of so many happy days."

"Happy days on your home planet?" I asked.

Mush came to Earth from a planet known as Growf-Woof-Woof, where she had a little girl as a pet.

"Yes," Mush said.

"Do you miss Growf-Woof-Woof?"

"Of course, I miss it sometimes," Mush said. "But this is a very nice planet, and you are a very nice friend."

"I wish you'd tell me more about your planet, and how you happened to come to this one."

"Well, it's such a long story," Mush said.

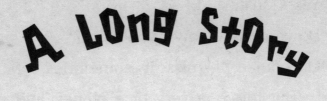

A Long Story

"**I** like long stories."

"Very well," Mush said. "I will tell you. May I pour another cupful of lemonade?"

"Please," I said, and settled down to listen.

"Growf-Woof-Woof is a planet much like this one, except of course that dogs are the top animals, which is as it should be—and Man is Dog's best friend. Life is pleasant on Growf-Woof-Woof. We are quite civilized, as you must have noticed. We are peaceful dogs: we cultivate the arts, have fair laws, enjoy nature—and there are some quite good restaurants."

"Were you a chef on Growf-Woof-Woof?" I asked.

"Kelly, I was president of the whole planet."

"Really?"

"Yes. But cooking was my hobby."

"You are a very good cook. You could have been a chef if you had wanted to."

"Thank you."

"Please continue with your story. How did you happen to come to Earth?"

"Perfectly simple," Mush said. "One day I felt like taking a little excursion. I felt like exploring. I started out with no destination in mind. I saw all sorts of interesting things, like asteroids, comets, solar systems, and planets."

"Did you go in a spaceship?" I asked.

"A little one."

"And you got farther and farther from your home planet?" I asked.

"Yes."

"And you couldn't remember the way back?"

"No."

"So, you were lost."

"Yes."

"Poor doggie," I said.

"Scratch behind my ears," Mush said.

Crashed!

"And you crashed on Earth?" I asked.

"Ran out of gas," Mush said.

"Spaceships run on gas?"

"Yes."

"You ran out of gas?"

"Then I crashed."

"Ruined the spaceship?"

"Totally."

"Then what happened?" I asked.

"Well, I was sort of lying by the side of the road, thinking. I was thinking about how I was stuck on some planet I had never heard of, with no way to go home. Then this donkey came along."

"A donkey?"

"Yes. He was running away from home. He had an idea that he wanted to be a musician.

"'I am going to the city to become a musician,' the donkey said. 'You can come with me and be a musician too.'

"'What city?' I asked.

"'Chicago,' the donkey said. 'What instrument would you like to play?'

"'Saxophone,' I said.

"'So, come with me,' the donkey said.

"'Why not?' I said.

"The donkey and I walked along the road. I forgot to mention to you that I had my saxophone with me in the spaceship. I like to play while I travel. In fact, that's how I happened to get lost. I must not have been paying attention."

"What instrument did the donkey play?" I asked Mush.

"Trombone. So the donkey and I are walking along, and we come across this cat, going down the road, dragging a banjo.

"'Excuse me,' the donkey says. 'Are you by any chance running away from home and going to Chicago to be a musician?'

"'What are you,' the cat asked, 'a mind reader?'

"'It's just that my friend, the dog, and I, are going to Chicago to be musicians ourselves.'

"'What a coincidence,' the cat said.

"'Isn't it?' the donkey said. 'So, we were wondering if maybe you'd like to come with us.'

"'Well, I don't mind if I do,' said the cat.

"So there we were, the donkey, the cat, and myself, walking along the road and talking about Chicago.

"'You know, what we need for our band is a girl singer,' the donkey said.

"'Yes, someone glamorous, with a good voice,' the cat said.

"'Of course, I have to play the saxophone, or I would do it,' I said.

"'Well, we need you to play the saxophone,' the donkey said.

"Night was coming, so we stopped to rest at an abandoned gas station. I had some sandwiches I had taken from my spaceship, and I shared them with the donkey and the cat.

"'Let's practice and get some tunes ready for when we get to Chicago,' the donkey said.

"We got out our instruments and began to play. We sounded good. We tried a number of tunes. The best one was 'Black Snake Moan,' and the donkey played a very fine trombone solo.

"We were feeling pleased with ourselves. We were a good band. After playing 'Black Snake Moan,' we played 'Muskrat Ramble.' The cat was very good on the banjo.

"When we were playing, 'Three Little Fishies in an Itty-bitty Poo',' we heard something wonderful. It was a voice, singing along. It sounded so good.

"'Where is that voice coming from?' the cat asked.

"'Who is singing?' the donkey asked.

"It was a chicken, sitting in a tree. When we had finished playing, we asked her, 'Will you come to Chicago with us and be the singer with our band?'

"The chicken said she would think about it.

"In the morning, when we started out along

the road, the chicken was with us. She was coming to Chicago with us, to sing with our band."

Chicago

★

"**D**id you get to Chicago? What happened next?" I asked Mush.

"When we arrived in Chicago, we got a job playing in a place by the lake, where they sold ice cream, and people danced. The name of the place was Tutti Frutti's Pleasure Palace. We were a big success. Crowds of people came to hear us. The name of our band was 'The Hot Animals.' We made lots of money and lived in the Drake Hotel. We went

everywhere in taxicabs and had our pictures in the newspaper.

"The owner of the ice cream parlor and dance hall where we worked was a rough character named Scooper John. He had a broken nose and a gold tooth, and it was said he'd been sent to prison for beating up a gorilla. He was a bad man, but he had a big heart.

"Some of Scooper John's friends were not very nice. They would come to Tutti Frutti's and say rude things while we were playing, and dribble ice cream on their expensive suits. When they were in a playful mood, they would take out big pistols and shoot holes in the ceiling. To tell the truth, we were a little afraid of them. We suspected they were robbers.

"One night the cat heard Scooper John's rough friends talking. They were planning to come to Tutti Frutti's late at night, after everyone had gone home. They were going to take all the ice cream away in a truck and also steal the money.

"'We should tell Scooper John,' the cat said.

"'Better not,' the donkey said. 'You know what a bad temper Scooper John has. There would be a fight.'

"'We could tell the police,' the chicken said.

"'Scooper John is allergic to the police,' the donkey said.

"'What can we do?' the cat asked. 'We can't just leave our boss to the mercy of these robbers.'

"'We need to make a plan,' I said. 'Where did you hear them talking, Cat?'

"'In the men's room. They were trying to sponge ice cream out of their loud and tasteless neckties.'

"'Are they still in there, sponging?'

"'I think so.'

"'This is what we must do. You, Chicken, and you, Cat, go at once. Stand near the door of the men's room and whisper loudly.'

"'Whisper loudly?'

"'Yes. Whisper loudly to each other. Be sure the robbers can hear you. They must think they are overhearing a whispered conversation. They must believe what they hear. And there is nothing as sincere as a whispering chicken.'

"'What do we whisper?' asked the cat."

Haunted!

"**T**his is what the cat and the chicken whispered, outside the men's room door. This is what the robbers, inside the men's room, trying to sponge the ice cream out of their loud and tasteless neckties, heard:

Cat: Haunted.

Chicken: Haunted?

Cat: Oh, haunted for sure.

Chicken: With ghosts, haunted?

Cat: Ghosts and spirits.

Chicken: Friendly ones?

Cat: Definitely not friendly.

Chicken: Are you sure?

Cat: Cats know these things.

Chicken: When do they come?

Cat: They come at night.

Chicken: What do they do?

Cat: They make strange music.

Chicken: What happens next?

Cat: Too horrible.

Chicken: Too horrible to tell?

Cat: Too horrible to think about."

"Robbers are always afraid of ghosts, aren't they?" I asked Mush.

"Yes, Kelly," Mush said. "They always are."

THUMPTHUMPTHUMP
THUMPTHUMPTHUMP

★ ★ ★

"That night, when Tutti Frutti's closed, we did not go home. We hid in the cellar and waited. It was dark in the basement, and scary. There were spiders. We were very quiet. We didn't make a sound. It seemed to us that we were there for a very long time. We wondered if the robbers were going to come.

"We waited in the dark.

"We waited.

"And waited.

"We waited some more.

"'My beak itches,' the chicken said.

"'Shhh!' we all said.

"'I have to go to the bathroom,' the cat said.

"'Shhh!' we all said.

"Then we heard the robbers talking.

"'What if there are ghosts?' one robber said.

"'There are no ghosts,' another robber said.

"'I am scared of ghosts,' the first robber said.

"'So am I,' another robber said.

"'Who ever heard of ghosts in an ice cream parlor and dance hall?' we heard the robber who had said there are no ghosts say.

"'If there are ghosts, I am going,' we heard a robber say.

"'If there are ghosts, I am gone,' we heard another robber say.

"'If there are ghosts, I was never here in the first place,' a third robber said.

"We got out our instruments. The donkey put a mute in the bell of his trombone. I put a hat over the bell of my saxophone. The cat put a pair of socks in his banjo. The donkey gave us the nod, and we began to play.

"We played very softly. We played so softly, we could barely hear ourselves. We played 'Black Snake Moan.'

"We could hear the robbers thumping.

"We played ever so slightly louder.

"The thumping stopped.

"'Do you hear music?' a robber asked.

"'Ghostly music!' another robber said.

"We played a tiny bit louder.

"'Oh, Mommy! It's ghosts!' a robber said.

"We played louder.

"'Ghosts!' a robber screamed.

"We heard *thump. Thump, thump, thump, thump, thump, thumpthumpthumpthumpthump thump.*

"The robbers were running.

"The donkey pulled the mute out of his trombone. The cat pulled the socks out of his banjo. I took the hat off the bell of my saxophone. The chicken threw her head back and sang 'Black Snake Moan' as loud as she could.

"*Crash!* We heard the back door slam."

Time to Bake the Pie

★ ★ ★

"And that was how we saved our boss, Scooper John, from having his ice cream and money stolen by robbers."

"What happened after that?" I asked Mush.

"The band broke up. We went our different ways. The donkey went to New York, the chicken went to Hollywood to be in the movies. The cat stayed with Scooper John, and I went to work inventing things. I had lots of different adventures."

"What sorts of adventures?" I asked.

"All sorts. But now we have to go home and start cooking supper. Your parents will be home before long. There are eggplants to peel, tomatoes to chop, and potatoes to roast, and there's just enough time to bake the pie."

"Will you tell me more stories about your adventures on this planet?" I asked Mush.

"Yes, another time," Mush said.

COBBLE · STREET

has never
been this much fun!

**Join Lily, Tess, and Rosie on their adventures
from Newbery Medalist Cynthia Rylant:**

The Cobble Street Cousins: In Aunt Lucy's Kitchen
0-689-81708-8
US $3.99/$5.50 CAN

The Cobble Street Cousins: A Little Shopping
0-689-81709-6
US $3.99/$5.50 CAN

The Cobble Street Cousins: Special Gifts
0-689-81715-0
US $3.99/$5.50 CAN

The Cobble Street Cousins: Some Good News
0-689-81712-6
US $3.99/$5.50 CAN

The Cobble Street Cousins: Summer Party
0-689-83417-9
US $3.99/$5.50 CAN

And coming soon from Aladdin Paperbacks:

The Cobble Street Cousins: Wedding Flowers
0-689-83418-7
US $3.99/$5.50 CAN